THE WIZARD TRILOGY

Jean Ure was six when she wrote her first book and still at school when her first novel was published. Since then, she has written numerous popular titles for young people, including the *Woodside School Stories; A Proper Little Nooryeff; Hi There, Supermouse!; The You-Two; The Unknown Planet* and *Captain Cranko and the Crybaby.* She has written three stories about the twins and Ben-Muzzy, *The Wizard in the Woods, Wizard in Wonderland* and *The Wizard and the Witch.* She first had the idea for the Wizard Trilogy several years ago and has been waiting for an opportunity to write it ever since. She lives in Surrey with her husband, six dogs and two cats.

Books by the same author

A Dream Come True
Cool Simon
Hi There, Supermouse!
Star Turn
The Wizard in the Woods
Wizard in Wonderland

For older readers

Always Sebastian
If It Weren't For Sebastian
One Green Leaf
The Other Side of the Fence
Plague Trilogy
(Plague 99, Come Windy April,
Watchers at the Shrine)
A Proper Little Nooryeff
You Win Some, You Lose Some